Fashion Fairy Princess

With fairy big thanks to Catherine Coe

First published in the UK in 2014 by Scholastic Children's Books
An imprint of Scholastic Ltd
Euston House, 24 Eversholt Street
London, NW1 1DB, UK
Registered office: Westfield Road, Southam, Warwickshire, CV47 0RA
SCHOLASTIC and associated logos are trademarks and/or registered
trademarks of Scholastic Inc.

Text copyright © Scholastic Ltd, 2014
Cover copyright © Pixie Potts, Beehive Illustration Agency, 2014
Inside illustration copyright © David Shephard, The Bright Agency, 2014

The right of Poppy Collins to be identified as the author
of this work has been asserted by her.

ISBN 978 1407 13953 1

A CIP catalogue record for this book is available from the British Library.

Printed and bound by CPI Group (UK) Ltd, Croydon, CR0 4YY
Papers used by Scholastic Children's Books are made
from wood grown in sustainable forests.

1 3 5 7 9 10 8 6 4 2

This is a work of fiction. Names, characters, places,
incidents and dialogues are products of the author's imagination
or are used fictitiously. Any resemblance to actual people, living
or dead, events or locales is entirely coincidental.

www.scholastic.co.uk
www.fashionfairyprincess.com

Fashion Fairy Princess

Rosa

🔒 in Sparkle City 🔒

POPPY COLLINS

■SCHOLASTIC

Dream
Mountain

Jewel Forest

Sparkle
City

Star
Valley

River
Sapphire

Shimmer Island

Glitter Ocean

Welcome to the world of the fashion fairy princesses! Join Rosa and friends on their magical adventures in fairyland.

They can't wait to visit

Sparkle City!

Can you?

Chapter 1

KNOCK KNOCK! Rosa jumped
up from her pink glass dressing
table, where she'd been
combing her long dark
hair, and fluttered over
to the bedroom
door. Who could
it be? She guessed
it was one of her

three best friends, but it was early on a Saturday morning, and Rosa was almost always the first fashion fairy princess to wake up.

She twisted the rose-shaped doorknob and slowly opened the door.

"Good morning, Princess Rosa," said a tiny double-winged fairy-helper who stood in the palace corridor. "Your presence is required in the Royal Hall. Please hurry – the king and queen are waiting for you." With that, the dainty fairy flew off to her next errand, her wings fluttering so fast she became just a blur.

Rosa's mouth dropped open in surprise – why did the fairy king and queen want to see her? But there was no time to worry about that! The fairy princess quickly changed from her pink cotton nightgown into a fuchsia bell skirt and a strawberry-print top. She hoped it was smart enough for the fairy king and queen. They lived in a separate wing of Glimmershine Palace, which they didn't leave very often, as the king was old and rather frail. It meant the fairy princesses rarely saw them, so Rosa knew this must be something important. She pulled her long hair into a high ponytail, slipped on her favourite pink sparkly shoes and adjusted her dark-rimmed glasses to complete her look, then she rushed out to the hallway.

"Rosa! We were just coming to get you!" said Bluebell. The fashion fairy princess was fluttering in the corridor next to Rosa's two other best friends, Buttercup and Violet.

"Did you get the message?" asked

Violet, her brown eyes bright with excitement.

Rosa nodded. "Yes!" she replied. "We'd better hurry!"

One after the other, the four fashion fairy princesses flew as quickly as they could along the white marble hallway. They fluttered down the sweeping glass staircase without putting so much as a foot on a step. At the bottom of the stairs, they spun round in the diamond-tiled entrance hall and then sped off along the ground-floor corridor to the right. This led to the king and queen's wing of

Glimmershine Palace, past walls that were filled with magical portraits of all the past fairy kings and queens. When she was little, Rosa spent hours in this hallway just looking at the beautiful pictures. She secretly hoped she might become the fairy queen one day.

The corridor began to widen, and the fairy princesses soon saw a huge arched golden door, guarded by a tall, golden-feathered cockerel. "Cock-a-doodle-doo!" it cried in a loud, ringing voice.

Rosa looked round at her three friends. She suddenly felt very nervous!

Fortunately, nothing seemed to scare Violet. She had already stepped forward, pushing the heavy golden door with one hand. The other fashion fairy princesses shuffled along behind her, letting out gasps as they took in the

Royal Hall. They'd been there before, on very special occasions, but the room still took their breath away. It was enormous, with a sparkling glass domed roof. The bright fairyland sunshine that poured through it made everything in the hall glisten – especially the jewel-covered walls and silver-stone floor.

Along both the right and left walls stood the cutest pink fairy-bunnies Rosa had ever seen, each with miniature wings and holding tiny trumpets. She noticed that at the end of the Royal Hall, the two ruby thrones were empty. The fairy princesses waited, not daring to move a muscle.

Suddenly, the fairy-bunnies brought their trumpets to their mouths. They chorused a short rising melody that was both beautiful and important-sounding. The four friends grabbed each other's

hands tightly, and as the bunnies lowered their trumpets, in came the fairy king and queen through an arch at the back of the hall.

The fairy royalty wore matching blue-sequinned cloaks, their sky-blue wings just visible under them. The queen's thick blonde hair was topped with a delicate gold tiara, while the king wore an eight-pointed golden crown. They fluttered in slowly, the king helping himself along with a pearl-topped walking stick. The fairies watched in silence as the pair lowered themselves on to their ruby thrones.

"Hello, fairy princesses," the fairy king began in a deep voice. The four friends curtseyed deeply.

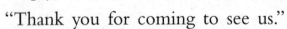

"Thank you for coming to see us."

Rosa relaxed her grip on Buttercup's hand. The king didn't sound very scary at all.

"We have something very important

to ask of you," the queen continued in a light, musical voice. Her beautiful green eyes glittered as she spoke. "We know how talented you fairy princesses are, especially when it comes to fashion. And so we'd like you to put on a fashion show for us."

Rosa's heart leapt – how exciting!

"But this is no ordinary fashion show," said the king. "It will be to celebrate our golden jubilee tomorrow. We'd like it to be extra special to mark our fifty years as fairy king and queen."

"Not only that, but your designs will make up the next season's fashion in Sparkle City," said the queen. "So it's also important to design outfits that everyone here will love."

"So, will you do it?" the king asked.

"Yes, Your Majesties," replied the four

friends in unison as they curtseyed again.

"We will do our very, very best," added Violet.

The king's face broke into a huge beam. "Thank you, fairy princesses," he said.

The queen nodded. "We cannot wait to see your fashion fairy creations!"

Chapter 2

"What do you think of this?"
Bluebell asked.

The four friends
were gathered around
a large glass table
in the palace's
craft studio,
Studio
Sublime.

They usually spent time together in one of their own wings of the palace, but this task was too important for that. They needed lots of space! The studio took up the whole of the fifth floor of the palace and had floor-to-ceiling windows, which let in the magical fairyland sunlight. Stretched across the ceiling hung threads of moth-silk on which they could pin up paper, or materials, or entire outfits. Bluebell was holding up a large sketchpad that was covered in doodles.

"Or this one?" She turned the page to a sunshine-yellow summer dress.

Buttercup smiled – yellow was her favourite colour. "Could it be made of yellow daffodil petals, with beeswax buttons and a buttercup-petal trim?"

"That sounds wonderful," Rosa said. "But do you think we'll be able to design the outfits in time? We only have one day to plan everything."

"I'm worried," said Violet with a frown. "It's tomorrow, and there's so much to do!"

Just then, the glass door of the studio burst open, and a green-winged fairy-helper flew in.

"I found these for you in the basement," she said in a squeaky voice, holding up a great pile of fabric that shimmered with fairy magic.

"Thank you ever so much," Rosa said, fluttering over to meet the little fairy and take the piles of fabric that weighed her down. But instead of the helper flying off quickly as usual, she remained on the spot.

"There was something else," she began quietly. "The fairy king and queen have sent you a special mirror-gram." The fairy-helper reached into a little velvet bag that was hooked on her arm. She brought out a mirror, as thin as the rice paper Buttercup used to decorate her delicious cupcakes.

The helper held it out towards the fashion fairy princesses, and they crowded round it, peering in.

At first all Rosa could see was their own reflections in the mirror. But then clouds swam across the glass, and as they disappeared, the king and queen's faces became visible.

"We are sorry to disturb you again, fairy princesses," began the king.

"But there was something we forgot to tell you this morning," the queen continued. "We know this is a big task to ask of you, and so we want to make sure you're rewarded."

The king's grey eyes looked serious. "If the show is successful," he said, "we'd like to thank you by giving you a stone in Paradise Square."

"You'll be beside all the other fairies of Sparkle City who've done something special for us," added the queen. "Thank you, fairy princesses, for all you are doing for our jubilee."

Before anyone could reply, the vision in the mirror began to fade.

The fairy princesses looked at one another, reached out to hold hands and started jumping with excitement. Paradise Square – it was amazing! The square's pavements were engraved with the names of very important Sparkle City inhabitants – it was something very special indeed to have your name written there.

"Now we have to make sure our fashion show is amazing – it's got to be a catwalk extravaganza!" cried Rosa.

"I can't believe we've been given the chance to have our names placed in Paradise Square!" said Bluebell, spinning on the spot.

"Well, we must make sure we have an amazing grand finale. It wouldn't be a fashion show without one!" added Buttercup.

Violet was already pulling out the fabrics the fairy-helper had brought, throwing them on to the studio's tables.

"The problem is, how are we going to get it done in time?" Violet's long curly hair swung about as she waved different pieces of material in the air.

"Let's try not to panic," said Rosa, putting a hand on Violet's shoulder. "If we organize ourselves properly, I'm sure we can do it."

"Rosa's right," agreed Buttercup, blinking her blonde eyelashes.

"Hmm, let me think about this," said Rosa. She chewed on a pink glitter pencil, deep in thought.

Her friends waited in silence. Knowing how practical Rosa was, they could always rely on her to come up with a good solution.

"OK, I think the problem is that we're all here together. What we need to do is split up. That'll save us time," Rosa began. "As well as working on the designs in the studio, some of us need to go out shopping. We need to find inspiration and different pieces for our outfits."

"Great idea!" the others replied.

Rosa smiled. "Good. So how about Violet and I go shopping, while Bluebell and Buttercup stay here and work on the designs and fabric we already have?"

"It sounds like the perfect solution," said Bluebell.

"I agree!" cried Violet, grabbing Rosa by the arm. "Come on, let's go!"

"We won't be too long," Rosa called over her shoulder. *But in just one day,* thought Rosa, *will we be able to create fashions that everyone in Sparkle City will love, as well as designing outfits fit for a king and queen's jubilee?* Rosa crossed her fingers tightly as they flew out of the door. She hoped so!

Chapter 3

Rosa stopped at the door of the palace. "Can we borrow two shopping-storks, please?" she asked the fairy-helper who took care of the storks.

"Of course, Princess Rosa," she replied, and called two storks out of their nesting room.

The pale pink storks were the perfect shopping accessory. Rosa loved them – and not just because they were her favourite colour! The large birds each carried a giant net that held a lot more than two fairies would ever be able to carry!

The two fairy princesses flew over the cobbled palace drive, the shopping-storks close behind them. There was nothing that beat the feeling of flying, Rosa thought as she swept past the pony stables, the wild-flower meadow and the lily-pad lake. She beat her pink wings in the mild spring air and felt her long hair billowing behind her and the gentle sunshine warming her face.

Soon they were floating smoothly down on to Diamond Boulevard. It was the fairy princesses' favourite street, because it was full of fashion shops!

"Shall we start with Jewels and Gems?" Violet suggested. "We need lots of jewellery to accessorize the outfits."

Rosa nodded and ducked into the small arched doorway of the silver-fronted shop. The shopping-storks waited patiently outside.

Wind chimes tinkled gently as the two fairy princesses entered. Rosa grinned, even though she'd been in this shop hundreds of times before. It was magical, like being inside a giant jewellery box, with hundreds of gems hanging from the ceiling. They were threaded on to loops of silvery shimmer-shoot strands that grew in Twinkle Meadow.

"Hello, Rosa and Violet, what can I do for you?" smiled the red-headed fairy behind the counter. She was wearing so much jewellery it was hard to spot her – she blended into the shop like one giant gem.

"Hello, Ivy!" Violet greeted her.

"We're in a bit of a rush, I'm afraid," explained Rosa. "We're putting on a fashion show for the king and queen's jubilee, and we need some beautiful jewellery for our outfits. Can you help?"

"I most certainly can!" Ivy replied. She began rushing around the shop so fast that she became just a blur of sparkling colours.

Minutes later, Violet and Rosa were looking through the many necklaces, earrings, bracelets and rings that Ivy had picked out for them. There was a shiny oval-shaped ring, and when Violet tried it on it changed to lilac, the exact same colour as her pinafore dress. Then, as Rosa slipped it on her finger, it became hot pink – to match her fuchsia bell skirt.

"Amazing!" exclaimed Violet.

Then Ivy showed them a pair of dragonfly earrings. When Violet clipped them on, they came to life beneath each ear, fluttering as Violet turned her head to check them out in the mirror. There was also a heather-thread necklace, a pink-pearl tiara and a bracelet made of tiny ruby strawberries that smelled just like the fruit.

"We'll take them all!" Rosa decided, reaching into her pocket and passing Ivy several sparkling bags of fairy dust. Ivy grinned and popped the dust into a silver unicorn-bank on the counter.

"You'll come along to the show, won't you, Ivy?" Violet asked as they left the shop.

Ivy nodded. "Of course," she said. "In fact, would you like some help tomorrow? I'd love to be a fairy-stylist for you!"

"That would be wonderful, thank you!" cried Rosa, giving Ivy a hug.

Rosa could have stayed there for hours, but they had to get on! The two fairy princesses carefully placed the jewellery they'd bought into the shopping-storks' nets.

"Where next?" Violet asked.

But before Rosa could answer, she heard someone call her name.

"Rosa, it's you – hello!"

The fairy princess spun round. Behind her on the path were two pretty fairies – a petite blonde one dressed in a duck-egg-blue shirt dress and a fairy with curly auburn hair wearing a matching amber wrap-around dress.

"Holly, Summer, great to see you!" Rosa replied with a smile.

"Hi!" Violet joined in. "How are you? I'm sorry but we can't stop to chat – we're planning the jubilee fashion show and there's still *loads* to do!"

"No problem," Summer, the fairy wearing amber, replied. "But good luck – we're really looking forward to it!"

Summer and Holly began to flutter

into Jewels and Gems, but just as the
door-chime tinkled, Rosa cried, "Wait!"

The two fairies stuck their heads back
out of the shop. "Is everything OK?"
asked Holly.

"Yes, but I just had an idea," said Rosa.
"Would you two be models for us at the
show? We need more than just the four
of us, and you would be perfect!"

"Of course – we'd love to!" Summer was beaming.

"It would be a pleasure!" added Holly.

"Great, that's all set then. See you tomorrow!" Rosa zoomed up into the air, waving as she flew.

The shopping-storks and Violet were close behind her. They quickly flew to Magic Moments, a very special shop at the end of the boulevard, which specialized in enchantments for outfits.

"How about a Glow-Me-Up?" suggested the fairy owner, Opal, when Violet and Rosa explained about the fashion show.

"Perfect!" said Violet. It was a string of glow-worms which, when hung around a fairy's neck, would light up her entire outfit like a star.

The fairy princesses also bought

a halo hairpiece, a cancan skirt that danced with real bees, and wing-tip sparkles. They were delighted when Opal agreed to be a stylist for them too, and were soon on their way again. By now, the storks' nets were bulging with their shopping.

"Next stop, Sparkle Sensations!" Violet called. "We're sure to get some great inspiration there."

Moments later, the two fairy princesses stood in their favourite shop in the whole of Sparkle City, gazing in awe at the clothes that surrounded them. Sparkle Sensations was filled with every type of clothing you could imagine – from silk tops and lacy blouses to net skirts and ball gowns. Topaz, the owner, had arranged everything by colour so it was just like

being in a rainbow. Rosa spun round, taking in the red, orange, yellow, green, blue, indigo and violet.

"Hello, fairies," called Topaz from behind the counter, "let me know if you need any help, won't you?"

"Thanks, Topaz," said Rosa. "We're actually just here for some inspiration – we're putting on the jubilee fashion show tomorrow. I hope that's OK?"

"Absolutely – you are my best customers, after all!" Topaz grinned, and went back to serving a fairy-helper.

"Look, Violet, here's a satin bolero with lace sleeves," said Rosa. "We could make one in yellow spider-silk to go with the summer dress."

Violet nodded as she stroked a super-soft scarf. "And we could make a dandelion-seed scarf, perfect for chilly evenings."

"Brilliant idea!" Rosa clapped her hands, but then her smile vanished. "But we still don't have an amazing final piece to end the show. . ."

Violet suddenly turned to Rosa. "Oh dear! What in fairyland will we do?"

Chapter 4

Rosa and Violet could barely keep
their wings flapping as they returned
to Glimmershine Palace. They were
exhausted from their morning's shopping
in Diamond Boulevard, but at least the
shopping-storks' nets were completely
full of pieces to include in the fashion
show. They'd bumped into lots more of
their fairy friends, who they'd asked to

be models – and they'd all been excited about being in the show. And Rosa and Violet were so pleased that Topaz had agreed to be a fairy-stylist, along with Ivy and Opal.

"Let's go and get some starberry shakes for all of us, and then see how Buttercup and Bluebell are doing," suggested Violet.

Rosa thought that sounded like a wonderful idea – starberries were known for their wake-me-up qualities, and they really needed that right now!

They popped into the palace's kitchens, where the fairy-cook, Berry, slipped them four yummy clover cupcakes as well as the shakes. Then Rosa and Violet flew up to the fifth floor.

"How did you get on?" asked Bluebell. She was sketching in her notepad while

Buttercup spread waves of glorious fabric across each of the studio's tables.

"We got lots of stuff," said Violet as she shared the drinks and snacks around. "And we found models and stylists to help in the show."

"But we still don't know what we're doing for the final piece," Rosa added, rubbing her forehead.

Buttercup went over to one of the moth-silk threads and unpinned some outfits. "We've made these pink-edged denim dungarees, an orange-print blouse and a petal-bottomed chiffon maxi-dress." She whizzed over to the other side of the room. "And here's a five-layered frill skirt and a dip-dyed rainbow wrap dress. But I don't think any of them are right for the highlight of the show."

The fairies looked down, silent. The
outfits were gorgeous, but they needed
something particularly special.

"Come on." Bluebell jumped up from
the glass table. "We won't find a solution
like this. And we're the fashion fairy
princesses, after all – I'm sure we can
think of something!"

"Bluebell's right," Buttercup said softly,
although she couldn't help wringing her
hands. "We mustn't give up."

Rosa picked up Bluebell's sketchpad and turned it to a blank page. "How about a shower-sparkle brainstorm?"

The other fairies grinned. They liked the sound of that!

Bluebell pulled out a jar of shower-sparkles from a nearby cupboard. The fairy princesses sat themselves around one of the studio's large tables, Bluebell's sketchpad in the middle.

"Ready?" Bluebell asked, and the fairy princesses all nodded.

Bluebell unscrewed the jar carefully and flung up the contents over the centre of the table. The glistening sparkles hung in the air like spinning stars, and as the fairy princesses thought of ideas, they began to float down and settle on the sketchpad.

It was a magical sight as the four best friends' ideas landed on the page.

The sparkles formed glittering lines and colours – skirts, dresses, tops and blouses.

"Oooh, what's that?" Bluebell asked, her blue eyes alight. She pointed to a dress with a long train made up of too many layers to count.

"That's my idea," said Rosa. "I suddenly thought about a special jubilee dress with fifty different coloured layers of silk to represent the fifty years of the king and queen's rule. The silk would billow out in the air as the wearer flies."

The other fairy princesses smiled. It sounded magnificent!

Rosa was staring hard at the paper. "But I think it needs something else. . ."

"I know. How about fifty different jewels around the neckline?" said Violet. "They could reflect multicoloured lights all around the wearer!" The remaining shower-sparkles that were still floating in the air drifted down to depict the jewels on the dress.

"It's perfect!" said Bluebell and Buttercup together.

"The only problem is," said Rosa with a frown, "where do we find such enchanted jewels?"

Violet grinned. "Jewel Forest, of course!"

"You're right, and I'm sure the forest fairies would help us," Buttercup said shyly. "But do we have enough time? We'll never fly there and back in time for the show tomorrow."

"We could ask the royal butterflies to take us – it is an important errand, after all," said Bluebell.

Rosa was nodding. "But we need to get the dress and the other outfits made too. Why don't you and Violet go to fetch the jewels, and Buttercup and I will stay here?"

Violet grinned. "Good thinking!" she said, and she and Bluebell rushed off to the butterfly stables at the rear of the palace.

Moments later, through the large studio windows, Rosa watched Violet and Bluebell sail off on two gorgeous butterflies. Their soft purple wings beat steadily, soaring into the sky.

Rosa turned to Buttercup. "We might just make this fashion show the best ever," she said, her heart lifting with relief.

A knock at the door made the two friends jump. A little fairy-helper with ruby-red wings peered in. "A delivery for you," she called. "Actually, no, wait, *three* deliveries!"

The fairy princesses took the packages from the helper, who was almost completely hidden by the parcels. "What do you think they are?" Buttercup asked Rosa.

"There's only one way to find out!"
Rosa replied. She set down one of the
parcels on to a glass table and untied the
long green ribbon, which held together
an object wrapped in green crêpe paper.
"Oooh, pearl bracelets from the mermaids
in Glitter Ocean. The note says they
heard about the fashion show and sent
them specially. How sweet of them!"

Meanwhile, Buttercup was unwrapping
a small red box. "Shell earrings," she told
Rosa, "from the sand fairies on Shimmer
Island. They're gorgeous!"

The third package was the most impressive of all. It was wrapped with silver-threaded cream paper and tied with a piece of red silk. Inside was a beautiful beaded necklace from the dream fairies. "The note says the beads are made from stone buried deep inside Dream Mountain," said Rosa, "and that the rock beads will bring us good luck."

"I do hope so!" said Buttercup as she began gathering silks for the dress.

They had such kind friends, Rosa thought, as she fluttered over to help Buttercup. Now that everything was coming together, she couldn't wait for the show!

Chapter 5

"That looks beautiful, Bluebell!" Rosa said admiringly. Her friend swirled around in a blue organza dress. The shimmering folds rested perfectly on the floor.

"Thanks, Rosa," said Bluebell, grinning in front of the studio's mirrors. The mirrors were angled in such a way that she could see every side of herself. It also made it seem like there were at least six

of her! "Can you pass me the lavender corsage from the table?"

Rosa put down the outfit she was working on and plucked up the tiny piece of lavender, which was tied tightly with a piece of ribbon. She took a sniff as she passed it to Bluebell. It smelled wonderful – the lavender was sweet and soothing. "Wow," Rosa breathed.

"On the way home from Jewel Forest, we found a whole bunch of lavender bushes in Pickleput Orchard," Violet explained, and then winked. "And I may have added just a touch of fairy magic to make the scent last!"

Just after lunch, Violet and Bluebell had brought back the fifty jewels they needed from Jewel Forest, and Rosa had spent the whole afternoon using glitter glue to stick them to the gorgeous, multicoloured jubilee dress. Her fingers were sore, but she still had lots of the jewels to glue on! Meanwhile the other fairy princesses had to make a few finishing touches and then they could get an early night – ready for the big show the following day.

"That's the dandelion-seed scarf done," announced Buttercup, hanging it up on the moth-silk thread above her.

"And this is finished too!" Violet was holding up a stylish purple tweed jacket and shorts suit which had honeysuckle flowers dotted on the collar, sleeves and cuffs.

Rosa had her tongue stuck out in concentration. "Just this one last jewel to go," she said finally, gripping a tiny ruby in a pair of wishbone tweezers. "There, finished!"

The four fashion fairy princesses stood back and looked at all their creations filling up Studio Sublime. What an honour it would be to show them all off tomorrow! All the outfits looked fantastic, but the fairy princesses agreed that the final jubilee dress was simply breathtaking.

"I love how all the jewels light up the studio!" said Bluebell as the others all nodded.

Rosa felt a warm glow of pride. *It was*

worth spending all those hours gluing them on, she thought.

"We should get to bed," Rosa said, taking one last look at the dress over her shoulder before turning off the lights.

Even in the darkness the jewels from the dress shone like stars.

Tap, tap! Tap, tap!

Rosa sat up in bed. She'd been trying to get to sleep for hours, but all she could think about was the fashion show.

"Who is it?" she called.

"It's me, Violet." The fairy princess's dark curly hair poked around the door.

"And me."

"Me three!"

Rosa blinked as Bluebell's brown bobbed head appeared below Violet's and then Buttercup's head popped up above.

"We're way too excited to sleep," Violet explained as the three 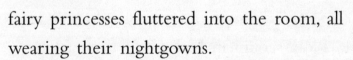 fairy princesses fluttered into the room, all wearing their nightgowns.

"My mind's full of fabrics and outfits and jewellery!" added Bluebell.

Rosa couldn't help but grin at her friends. "I feel the same, but we have to at least *try* to get some sleep before tomorrow."

Buttercup perched on the corner of Rosa's pink four-poster bed. "I thought we might go for a walk," she said in her soft, feathery voice. "It might help calm us down."

Suddenly a walk seemed like the perfect idea, and by the look of the sky through Rosa's window, it was a lovely mild evening. She jumped out of bed, wrapping her pink cloud-cotton nightgown around her heart-print pyjamas. "You're right – let's go!" she agreed.

The fairy princesses were soon skipping through the palace's glittering doors and along the cobbled drive.

"Perhaps we could go and see the catwalk in Paradise Square," Buttercup suggested as they all linked arms and stepped daintily over the stones. The fairy princesses loved to fly, but sometimes it was nice to slow down and walk together.

"Oooh, yes, it should be up by now," said Violet.

"Look there – I think I can see it." Bluebell was pointing to something glistening in the distance.

As the four friends got closer, they could see just how majestic the fashion catwalk was. The long, delicate walkway was made entirely of crystal. As it caught the moonlight it made the whole of Paradise Square light up.

"It's magical," Rosa breathed.

"I bet it needed a giant heap of fairy magic!" said Violet, laughing.

Bluebell was tiptoeing across the pavement, looking down at the Paradise

Square stones – some empty, some filled
with fairy names. "Just imagine," she said.
"This time tomorrow, our names could be
here!"

"Oh, I do hope everyone likes our
outfits," said Buttercup.

"Do you know, I really think they will,"
Rosa said, putting her arms out to her friends.
The fairies stood silently for a moment,
their arms around each other, watching the
gentle glow of the beautiful catwalk.

As the moon's light began to fade, the fairies made their way back to Glimmershine Palace. The four best friends were all yawning as they reached the grand front door.

"Did you have a nice walk?" asked the fairy-helper at the door.

"Yes, thank you," Violet replied. "And now we're really ready for bed!"

"Would you like me to arrange for some daisy-milk to be brought to you?" the helper suggested.

"Yes, please!" the fairy princesses said at once.

It wasn't long before they were all tucked up in bed in their separate quarters, sipping hot, sweet daisy-milk from wing-handled butterfly mugs. Rosa put her empty mug on her cherry-tree nightstand and sank into her soft peacock-feather duvet. She drifted off to sleep, feeling calmer – and surer than ever that tomorrow's show would be as wonderful as they hoped.

Chapter 6

Rosa rubbed the sleep from her eyes and blinked at the bright sunshine flooding into her room. It was the day of the fashion show! She leapt out of bed and went over to her dressing table to tie back her long hair – it was already hot, and today would be a very busy day. Rosa remembered being exhausted last night, falling asleep as soon as her head touched the pillow – but this morning she felt rested and full of energy. It was the best night's sleep she'd ever had, she realized, thinking back to dreams of cupcakes and ponies and flying with her fairy princess friends. *It must have been the daisy-milk!* Rosa thought.

She dressed quickly – in some practical pink leggings and a butterfly-print shirt – and flew over to her window. Through the pink-tinted glass she saw fairy-stylists making their way to Paradise Square and little fairy-helpers rushing around on errands. The sky was dotted with hummingbirds carrying messages back and forth, and

the paths were full of carriages holding the fashion-show equipment. The whole of Sparkle City seemed to buzz with excitement – everyone was busy getting ready for the show. Speaking of which, she should do the same!

Rosa flew out of her wing of the palace and along the corridor. She knocked on Violet's, Buttercup's and Bluebell's doors in turn. Her friends sounded very sleepy – she guessed they'd slept just as deeply as she had – but soon they were all dressed and inside Studio Sublime.

"I still can't quite believe we're putting on a fashion show – today!" said Bluebell. "I so hope the king and queen will enjoy it."

"As well as everyone else in Sparkle City!" Violet reminded her.

Buttercup beckoned in several fairy-helpers, and went over to help them as they started gathering up the things they needed for the show.

"Let's get everything down to Paradise Square," Rosa directed. "Then we can work out which outfits we and all the other models will wear."

The fairy princesses gently unpegged the clothes, putting them all safely inside dress bags. Rosa took extra special care as she placed the jubilee dress inside a bag, making sure none of the jewels got caught on the layers.

"These are all for the fashion show," Bluebell said to the fairy-helpers. "The carriages at the palace entrance are waiting to take them."

The helpers nodded and flew out of the room with quick beats of their tiny wings.

Soon the studio was empty. The fairy princesses fluttered down the five flights of glass stairs inside the palace and skipped towards the last carriage that remained. They didn't want to fly, and tire themselves out for the show, especially as it was such a warm day.

The friends piled into the turquoise carriage and made themselves comfortable on the soft sponge cushions inside. "To Paradise Square!" Violet called to the matching turquoise-blue ponies at the front of the carriage. They whinnied, did a quick dance of their hooves, and with smooth flaps of their wings trotted off.

"Hurrah!" the fairies shouted as they zoomed along quickly. They were off to the show!

Rosa felt her heart skip a beat as they

approached Paradise Square. It looked
completely different from last night –
now it was full of fairies and helpers
getting everything ready. In the hot
bright sunshine, the crystal catwalk had
a dazzling glow. The models and their
outfits would really shine on this, Rosa
thought!

As they emerged from the carriage,
the fairy princesses saw fairy-helpers
sprinkling fairy dust around the edges
of the square. Moments later, little white

toadstools began to spring up from the pavement.

"It's the seats for the audience!" Bluebell said, bouncing down on the one nearest to her and squealing with excitement as it sprang back to shape. "You should try them out," she said to her friends.

"They look great," Rosa said. "But we don't have time – we need to go and work out what each of us is wearing!" She fluttered towards a floating rainbow curtain that hid the far end of the catwalk. Through the curtain was the backstage dressing room – which looked far bigger than it did from the outside! Fairy magic, she guessed! Inside, all their outfits hung along one wall, and some of the fairy models were sitting next to each other, getting ready in front of mirrors.

Ivy, Opal and Topaz were combing the models' hair and polishing their wings. Everyone was chatting and smiling, the air filled with the sweet smell of flowery fairy-spray and shimmery wing-dust.

Rosa felt a shiver of excitement run down her spine. This was incredible – their very own fashion show!

Violet was already over by the

outfits. "I'm going to wear this one!" she said, pulling out the purple tweed jacket and shorts and holding them up against her. "I mean, if that's OK with everyone?"

Her friends nodded and smiled. Of course Violet should wear them – her favourite colour was purple, after all!

"It suits you perfectly," Buttercup said.

The fairy princesses began matching the outfits to the models, and soon there was just one outfit left – the final jubilee dress. Rosa held out the dress bag towards her friends.

"No, YOU have to wear that one," Bluebell said. "After all your hard work and organization, you deserve it.

Rosa started to shake her head, but her three friends were grinning.

"We insist!" Violet announced.

Now, Rosa's shivers of excitement had turned to waves. "Thank you," she said, feeling hot with anticipation. She fingered the dress bag. She knew she needed to sit down with a fairy-stylist but she couldn't help taking a peek at the beautiful outfit again first.

She brought out the dress slowly, the different coloured silk layers cool and smooth to the touch. But what was that tinkling sound? As Rosa looked down, her heart sank to her toes. The jewels were dropping from the dress like raindrops to the ground. It was ruined!

Chapter 7

"Oh no!" cried Rosa, staring at the dress in horror.

"What's happened!" shouted Violet over the noise of the preparations, rushing across to Rosa. She looked at the dress, and then saw the jewels scattered on the floor. "Oh my fairyness, it's a disaster!"

Buttercup and Bluebell flew over to join them. "Maybe it's not so bad.

Look, not all of them have fallen off," Buttercup said, pointing. But as Rosa looked closer at the jewelled neckline, another smattering of jewel-drops  sounded on the floor. There was only one jewel left, Rosa saw, an emerald one at the back of the neck, but just as she noticed it – *plop!* – the green jewel fell sadly to the ground.

Rosa felt tears pricking her eyes. "What are we going to do?" she said quietly. "The glue must have stopped working because it's such a hot day."

As Violet and Buttercup hugged Rosa, Bluebell bent down and started picking up the jewels from the floor.

"Could we use fairy magic to glue them back on?" Bluebell suggested.

Rosa shook her head. "I don't think it'd work," she said, "because the gems are already enchanted."

"I could go and explain what's happened to the king and queen?" Violet offered. "They'll understand. Maybe we could even postpone the show."

"I'm not sure about that," Buttercup replied slowly. "It's their jubilee – we can't disturb them now and spoil their day."

Rosa sighed, wiped her eyes with a daisy-petal hanky and tried to sound cheerful. "If we stand here worrying, none of the show will be ready in time. We'll just have to carry on without the final piece."

"If you're sure?" said Bluebell. The fairy princesses looked around. The room was full of fairy models in dressing gowns, their hair unpinned. There was still a lot to do.

"Yes," Rosa said, putting the dress back in its bag and forcing a smile. "We don't want to keep the king and queen – and the whole of Sparkle City – waiting, do we?"

Rosa tried to stop herself from shaking with disappointment as she went to check on the fairy-stylists. Ivy, Opal and Topaz were doing an amazing job – one of the fairies had a top-knot bun netted with the finest spider's web, and another had long flowing red curls that nestled perfectly on her auburn wings.

Buttercup was organizing the snacks that would be served to the audience during the show – the fairy princesses' favourites, cupcakes. What's more, they'd been decorated with icing in the shape of miniature handbags and shoes! As she carried out a cake stand, she sniffed them – toffee and butterscotch with a hint of honey. Yum!

Meanwhile, Bluebell helped the fairy models into their outfits. One wore the orange-print blouse and cancan skirt, another the rainbow wrap dress lit with Glow-Me-Up string. There was the petal-bottomed maxi-dress with the beaded rock necklace, and the pink-edged dungarees with dragonfly earrings. The models spun round, oohing and aahing at the sight of the gorgeous clothes.

As she fluttered around the dressing room, pinning a hem here, adding a ribbon there, Rosa could hear the excited chatting of the audience outside. Not long now! She was trying really hard not to think of the jubilee dress and how she wouldn't be able to take part in the show now that it was ruined. And she had been *so* looking forward to seeing the king and queen's faces when she modelled the special outfit for them. She thought back to all the hard work the fairy princesses had done to prepare for the fashion show. Designing the outfits, finding models and stylists, visiting the shops. . .

Wait! Rosa's mind had been so full of the show that she hadn't been able to think straight. But suddenly she had an idea. She might just be able to fix the dress after all!

"I've got to go," she told her fairy princess friends as she rushed to the door.

Bluebell, Buttercup and Violet swung round.

"But the show's about to begin!" Violet cried.

"I know – but I'll be as quick as I can," Rosa replied. "You might just have to start without me!"

Flapping her wings furiously, Rosa took off in the direction of Twinkle Meadow. With a tiny bit of fairy magic, her idea might just work!

Chapter 8

Rosa returned to Paradise Square just as the fairy-bunny trumpeters were announcing the arrival of the king and queen. Phew!

From the sky, Rosa could see that the square around the crystal catwalk was full of fairies – not just from Sparkle City, but from other fairylands too. Rosa beamed when she spotted Fern, one of the fairy princesses' best friends from Star Valley.

Fern was jumping up and down and waving. She looked gorgeous in a long, delicate orange maxi-skirt with chains of matching orange beads around her neck. And there was Honey – Rosa's cousin. She'd come all the way from Shimmer Island!

Rosa zoomed towards the floating rainbow curtain to join her fairy princess friends. Behind it the first models stood ready. Everyone fell silent as the fairy king and queen appeared on two crystal thrones at the head of the catwalk. You could hear fairy dust drop, it was so quiet, thought Rosa. Her wings tingled with excitement, knowing the show was just about to begin. This was it!

"Welcome, fairies," announced the king. "The fairy queen and I thank you for attending this fashion show to celebrate our jubilee."

"We're so looking forward to seeing the outfits, put together by our very own fashion fairy princesses, Rosa, Bluebell, Buttercup and Violet," the queen added.

The four fairy princesses stood nervously behind the rainbow curtain with the other models, waiting for the show to start. Rosa sneaked a peek through the curtain at the crowds of fairies and felt her tummy bubble with nerves. She *so* hoped everyone would like their designs!

"And now, let the show commence!"
The king stomped his walking stick on
the ground, and the fairy-bunnies began
playing a fast, fun melody.

"Buttercup, go!" Rosa said, and the
fairy princess fluttered through the
rainbow curtain and up on to the catwalk.
She wore the halo hairpiece and the
yellow daffodil summer dress – perfect for
a day like this, Rosa realized.

She held her breath as the king and queen and the hundreds of fairies in Paradise Square watched on. Rosa reached out and grasped Violet's hand tightly — her heart felt like it would leap out of her chest at any moment.

And then applause began to ripple around the square. Louder and louder it came, as more of the fairy models took to the glittering catwalk. *They like it!* thought Rosa.

Holly was up on the catwalk now, fluttering slowly along in the petal-bottomed strapless dress. The sunlight shining on the crystal walkway made everything glow and look extra magical. There was Violet in the purple suit with the strawberry bracelet and then Bluebell in the blue organza dress and shell earrings.

Rosa glanced at the fairy king and queen. They were clapping furiously too, with big smiles on their faces. She was so glad they were getting the jubilee show they had wanted – well, so far, anyway. But what about the final outfit? With moments to go before she had to appear in the jubilee dress, Rosa dashed into the dressing room.

"Rosa, you're next!" a fairy-helper called through the curtain.

Rosa took a deep breath, and flew out before she could change her mind. She fluttered up to the catwalk and took her first few steps along it. The fifty-layered dress was amazing to walk in. The silk train floated on the gentle breeze as if it were flying, and the layers rose and fell like little fabric wings.

On the

catwalk, Rosa felt like she had a hundred spotlights on her, such was the glow from the crystal walkway catching the sun. Her face ached from smiling – she couldn't stop grinning as the audience clapped harder than ever. And there were her three best friends watching from their places at the end of the catwalk – their eyes wide in surprise, beams across their faces. Rosa knew they'd be wondering how she'd fixed the fifty enchanted jewels to her dress – because there they were, sparkling around the neckline. Light bounced off them, splashing bright colours around Rosa as she gave a delicate twirl.

Then Rosa walked a few more steps to join all the other models at the end of the stage.

"How did you do it?" Bluebell

whispered to Rosa.

"I remembered seeing the loops of shimmer shoots in Jewels and Gems, and how their silvery stands held everything in place – and I suddenly realized that we could do the same with the jewels on the dress." Rosa glanced down. The shimmer-shoot threads wound around the jewels and caught the light like silk whiskers, making the dress look even more magical.

"But where did you find them?" asked Violet.

Rosa grinned. "In Twinkle Meadow of course! That's where all the shimmer-shoots grow." Rosa stopped talking, her voice drowned out by the roar of the crowd. The other models left the catwalk while the four fashion fairy princesses curtseyed to the king and queen. The king held his hand up for silence.

"Congratulations!" the king and queen boomed together.

"That was the most amazing fashion show Sparkle City has ever seen!" said the king.

"The outfits you designed were both spectacular and practical," the queen added. "I know we'll be seeing your designs on the Sparkle City streets very soon! And the final piece was stunning – a dress fit for a jubilee!"

"We haven't forgotten about your reward," said the king.

Rosa put her hand to her mouth – the Paradise Square stone! The king and queen may not have forgotten, but with everything that had happened, *she* had!

At the edge of the square, a dozen tiny fairy-helpers surrounded one of the pavement stones, covering it with a golden velvet veil.

"Don't be shy," said the queen. "Go and see it being revealed!"

The fairy princesses zoomed down to the pavement. They watched, speechless, as the helpers pulled the velvet cover away. Rosa caught her breath when she saw the words engraved into the stone in sparkling silver.

Congratulations to Rosa, Bluebell,
Buttercup and Violet

Sparkle City's
Four Fabulous Fashion
Fairy Princesses

The crowd applauded yet again as
the four friends joined in a group hug,
circling their Paradise Square stone.
"We did it!" cried Rosa. She looked
down at the sparkling words and a warm
glow of happiness flooded through her
that had nothing to do with the hot sun.
What a magical day it had been!

If you enjoyed this

Fashion Fairy Princess

book then why not visit our
magical new website!

- Explore the enchanted world of
  the fashion fairy princesses
- Find out which fairy princess
  you are
- Download sparkly screensavers
- Make your own tiara
- Colour in your own picture frame
  and much more!

fashionfairyprincess.com

Fashion Fairy Princess

Buttercup

in Glitter Ocean

Turn the page for a sneak peek of the next
Fashion Fairy Princess adventure...

Chapter 1

"Please could you pass me the petal pancakes, Buttercup?" asked Violet, eyeing the tall stack of fluffy pink cakes hungrily. "They look delicious."

"They are," said Bluebell, pouring rose-coloured syrup on to her second helping. "I think they might be the nicest I've ever tasted."

Buttercup passed the silver plate of

pancakes to her friend. It was a sunny Saturday morning and the fashion fairy princesses – Violet, Rosa, Buttercup and Bluebell – were having breakfast on the jewelled patio of Glimmershine Palace. All around them the glittering pink and purple flowers of the palace's gardens fluttered in the gentle breeze.

"It's such a beautiful day," said Buttercup, taking a sip of nectar from the flower-shaped glass in front of her. "I can't wait to get down to the palace stables."

"Oh look," said Violet, "here's Ferdinand with the fairy-mail. I wonder if he has anything exciting for me."

Ferdinand was a beautiful metallic blue firefly and a fairy-flyer. The fairy-flyers picked up and delivered the fashion fairy princesses' fairy-mail from all over Sparkle City.

Violet looked a little disappointed as Ferdinand buzzed quickly past her chair. He also passed Rosa and Bluebell but landed gently next to a surprised Buttercup.

"I wasn't expecting anything," said Buttercup excitedly as she thanked Ferdinand and reached into his saddlebag. When she pulled out her hand, she was holding a large gold glittering shell.

"What a beautiful shell," said Bluebell.

"It looks like it came from Glitter Ocean," said Rosa, peering closer. "Do you know someone from Glitter Ocean, Buttercup?"

"Only my Great-aunt Melinda. She's a mermaid and lives near Coral Castle with the other merpeople," answered Buttercup, examining the shell carefully, "but I haven't heard from her since last year's

Annual Fairy Festival."

"Aren't you going to open it?" said Violet, desperate to know what was inside. "Perhaps it's a present."

Buttercup looked at the large, flat shell in her hand and tried to open it with her delicate fingers, but nothing happened.

"Let me have a go," said Violet, reaching for the shell.

"Violet, it's Buttercup's invitation. Let her open it," said Rosa gently. "Buttercup, why don't you try using a little fairy-dust? Perhaps it was closed with fairy magic."

"Good idea, Rosa," said Violet. "Sorry, Buttercup, I was only trying to help."

Buttercup took out a small pouch of fairy-dust from the skirt of her dress and sprinkled a little over the shell. With a puff of golden glitter, the shell opened to reveal a shining yellow invitation. . .

Get creative with the fashion fairy princesses in these magical sticker-activity books!

And coming soon...